Mamie T

HARPER'S BRIGHT IDEA

Illustrations by Tamara DeStefano

Library of Congress Control Number: 2019905903

ISBN: 978-1-0710-9868-4

Published by Mamie Thomas · Florence, AL

Dedication

A heartfelt thank you to my six children who afforded me the inspiration and opportunity to write and publish this book. Many thanks to my husband who did not allow me to give up. Mary Marvella and Tamara DeStefano two exceptional individuals—editor and illustrator. Thank you both for equipping me with the knowledge and tools to move this book forward. I thank all of you for your guidance, patience and support. This process has been educational.

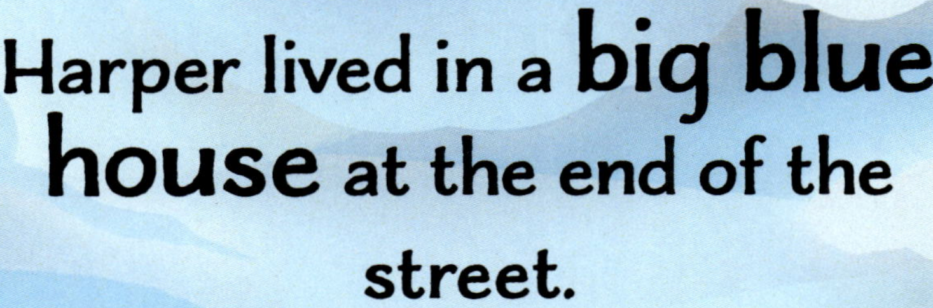

Harper lived in a **big blue house** at the end of the street.

Across the road was a **big empty field.**

Harper **loved** looking out of her upstairs bedroom window in the mornings.

She **loved** looking up at the sky and the bright sun. She **loved** looking into her backyard at the colorful flowers she and her mother planted.

But each time she looked across the road, she felt sad because the big field was **empty**.

This morning, Harper woke up early with a **big stretch** and a yawn.

Then, looking out her window she began to **smile**.

She had a BRIGHT IDEA!

Harper quickly dressed and then hurried to the kitchen.

"Good morning," her mom said as she set a plate of blueberry **pancakes** in front of Harper's chair.

"Thanks, Mom," Harper said.

With the bright idea in her mind, she ate her pancakes and syrup faster than ever before.

In between bites she asked, “Where can I find information on planting **trees and flowers** in that big empty field?”

Before her mom could answer she shouted, “I **know** who to call!”

She called the Waterloo Extension Service.

"My name is **Harper** and I live in the blue house at the end of Cleveland Avenue where there is a big empty field.

I want to make it **colorful** with plants. Can you tell me what kind of trees and flowers would be good to plant there?"

"Harper, my name is Mr. Gregoire. I know **exactly** which field you're talking about. Let me grab some brochures and I'll tell you about the many kinds of plants that will grow there."

Harper began to describe the kinds of trees she wanted. "I'd like trees that have sweet smelling flowers that bloom in the spring, like **Dogwood**.

And trees that grow fruit in the summer like **apples** and **plums**.

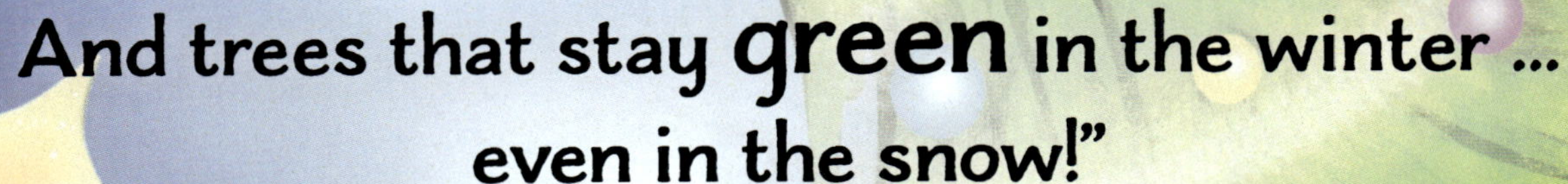

And trees that stay **green** in the winter ... even in the snow!"

Mr. Gregoire read a list of websites for Harper to look up. "Be sure to read them before you begin your project," he suggested.

She thanked him. This was just the information she needed to get this project started.

“Mom! Mom! Mr. Gregoire at the Waterloo Extension Service gave me some **great** ideas about making the empty field beautiful.”

“I’m going to plant **trees** and **flowers** there!”

"Well, that sounds like a lot of work for one person," her mother said. "Why don't you call a couple of **friends** or **cousins** to help you?"

Saturday morning the girls met at Harper's house to begin making **plans**.

Courtney asked Harper, "How do we get the **community** to help us?"

Jonah asked, "And do you know anyone who can help us make **fliers?**"

Harper's mom walked into the kitchen at that moment and said, "I'd be **glad** to help!"

And they got to **work**.

Please Come

Please come out and help
us plant trees and flowers
in the big field Saturday.
Bring your shovels and gloves.
The trees will clean the air,
mark the seasons, provide
shade and make our
neighborhood colorful!
If anyone would like to donate
trees or flowers, please call
Harper at
642-789-1251
Thank you!

Please Come

Harper suggested that each girl put fliers out on her own **street**.

Soon, phone calls came **pouring** in for her. Dad answered three in one evening! Mom suggested that she keep a journal of all donations.

The big day finally arrived. The sun was brightly **shining** and the wind was calmly blowing. Harper, Jonah and Courtney were the first to arrive at the field.

Mr. Gregoire's **green** truck pulled in right behind them.

Dad's red **truck** pulled up carrying all the trees and flowers that had been donated.

Harper ran to the truck to greet her dad and to see all the **plants**.

She picked up a small tree with **pink** blooms and asked, “Mr. Gregoire, is this a Cherry Blossom tree?”

Yes,” he replied, ”and it needs to be planted in **full sun.**” He pointed at a sunny spot and Harper grabbed a shovel to begin digging.

Once the hole was **deep** enough she carefully set the little tree in its place. Grinning, she covered the roots and gave the new tree a drink while Jonah took pictures.

Soon people arrived. Harper, Jonah and Courtney were **thrilled** to see so many. It seemed the entire community showed up to help.

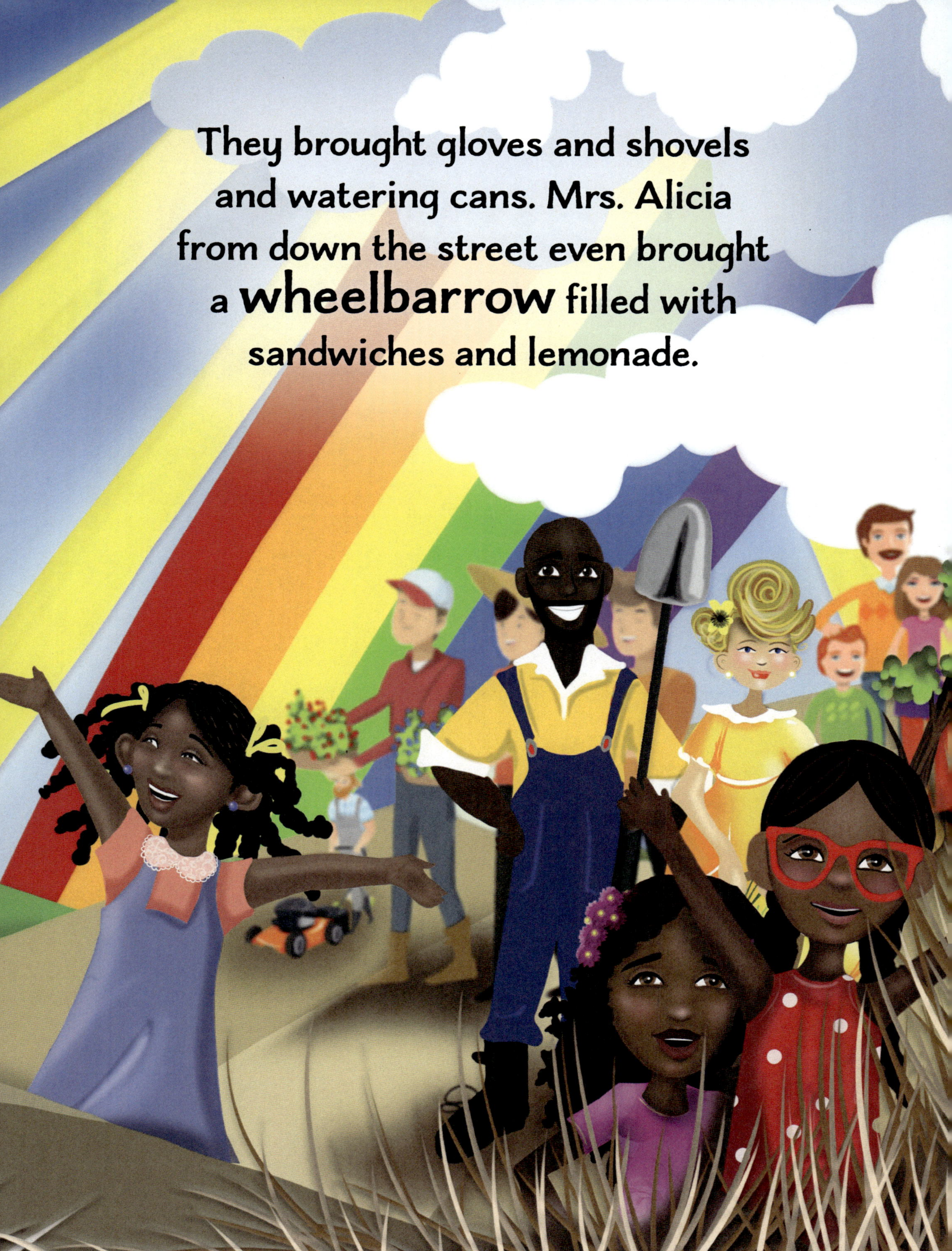

They brought gloves and shovels and watering cans. Mrs. Alicia from down the street even brought a **wheelbarrow** filled with sandwiches and lemonade.

Everyone got to work, **digging** holes and planting and watering and digging and digging and planting and watering!

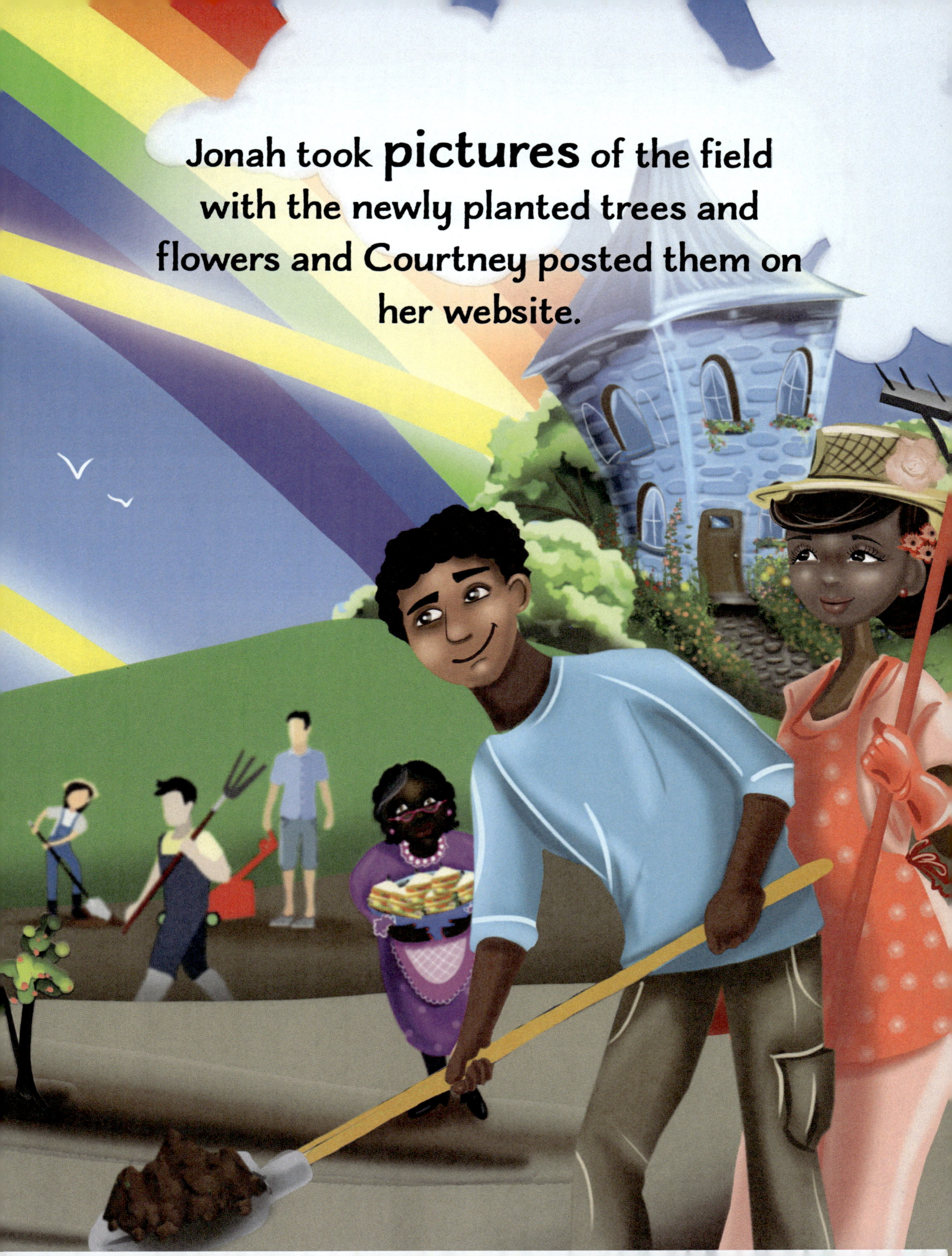

Jonah took **pictures** of the field with the newly planted trees and flowers and Courtney posted them on her website.

Soon the field looked very different.

Harper stood in front of the people who had come to help. "Thank you for helping and donating all of the wonderful plants. By next **summer** this field will be in full bloom and we'll all be able to enjoy the colorful and sweet smelling trees and flowers we planted."

With the help of an adult, contact your local extension service to learn about your state tree and flower.

DRAW YOUR FLOWER HERE:

My State

My State Tree

My State Flower

About the Author:

Mamie Thomas has been an educator of young children since her teenage years. Educated in the Alabama public school system, she completed her studies at Tuskegee University.

She owned and operated a preschool for 10 years. The love for inspiring children to be all they could be took its roots here. She greeted each of them daily with a warm smile, a hot breakfast and a book. Many children had the opportunity to begin their early educational endeavors at First Step PreSchool in Florence, Alabama.

In 2001 she began to work as a mentor with the Family Child Care Partnership at Auburn University. She continues to work in this field training child home care providers to achieve excellence in their chosen profession.

About the Illustrator:

Tamara DeStefano is an artist and dreamer who has been creating colorful characters and whimsical backdrops since she was a little girl. A freeleance illustrator and published author, Tamara lives in Atlanta. She loves hearing from readers. Follow her on Instagram @tamaradestefanoart

About the Editor:

Mary Marvella, a Georgia native, has been telling stories since the days she waited for the bookmobile instead of the ice cream truck. She made up the games her friends played for Let's pretend and Play like... Now she writes, edits and tutors English. She enjoys editing and polishing stories.

Mary has published 10 novels and novellas.

Made in the USA
Columbia, SC
18 April 2023